Princess Ponies

A Magical Friend

With special thanks to Julie Sykes

Bloomsbury Publishing, London, New Delhi, New York and Sydney

First published in Great Britain in March 2013 by Bloomsbury Publishing Plc
50 Bedford Square, London WC1B 3DP

www.bloomsbury.com
www.ChloeRyder.com

Bloomsbury is a registered trademark of Bloomsbury Publishing Plc

Text copyright © Awesome Media and Entertainment Ltd 2013
Illustrations copyright © Jennifer Miles 2013

The moral rights of the author and illustrator have been asserted

A CIP catalogue record for this book is available from the British Library

ISBN 978 1 4088 2727 7

Typeset by Hewer Text UK Ltd, Edinburgh
Printed and bound in Great Britain by CPI Group (UK) Ltd, Croydon CR0 4YY

7 9 10 8

Princess Ponies ♡

A Magical Friend

CHLOE RYDER

BLOOMSBURY
LONDON   NEW DELHI   NEW YORK   SYDNEY

The Pony

Queen
Moonshine

Princess
Crystal

Princess
Cloud

Princess
Stardust

Princess
Honey

Royal Family

King
Firestar

Prince
Jet

Prince
Comet

Prince
Storm

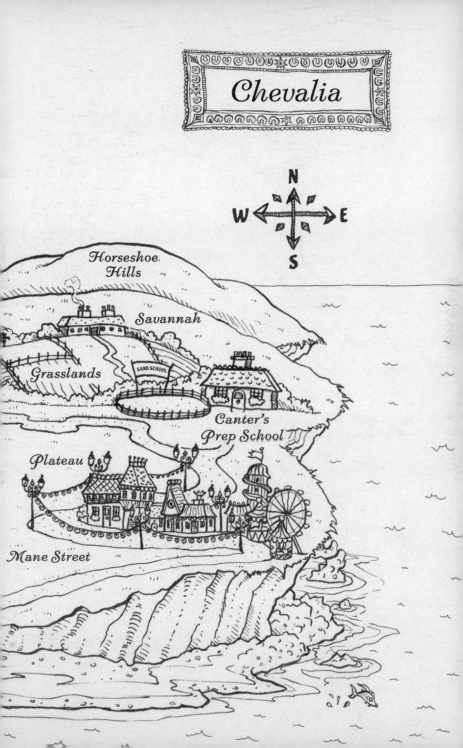

Early one morning, just before dawn, two ponies stood in an ancient court-yard, looking sadly at a bare stone wall.

'In all my life this wall has never been empty. I can't believe that the horse-shoes have been taken — and just before Midsummer Day too,' said the stallion.

He was a handsome animal — a copper-coloured pony, with strong legs and bright eyes, dressed in a royal red sash.

The mare was a dainty yet majestic palomino with a golden coat and a pure white tail that fell to the ground like a waterfall.

She whinnied softly. 'We have so little time to find them all.'

With growing sadness the two ponies watched the night fade away and the sun rise. When the first ray of sunlight spread into the courtyard it lit up the wall, showing the imprints where the golden horseshoes should have been hanging.

'Midsummer Day is the longest day of the year,' said the stallion quietly. 'It's the time when our ancient horseshoes must renew their magical energy. If the horseshoes are still missing in eight days, then by nightfall on the eighth day, their magic will fade and our beautiful island will be no more.'

Sighing heavily, he touched his nose to his Queen's.

'Only a miracle can save us now,' he said.

The Queen dipped her head regally, the diamonds on her crown sparkling in the early morning light.

'Have faith,' she said gently. 'I sense that a miracle is coming.'

Chapter 1

Pippa MacDonald turned her pony, Snowdrop, towards the last jump, a solid-looking red and white wall. Snowdrop pricked up her ears and, snorting with excitement, she sped up.

'Steady, girl,' Pippa said, checking her with the reins.

None of the other riders had ridden a clear round. Pippa and Snowdrop were the last to go and if they cleared the wall they would win the competition, taking home a silver cup and a red rosette. As the wall came closer, Pippa forced back the nervous, fluttery feeling growing in her stomach.

'We can do this,' she whispered to Snowdrop.

She leaned forward, standing up in her stirrups, loosening the reins to give Snowdrop her head as she pushed her pony into the jump. Snowdrop leapt over it eagerly, carrying Pippa upwards. For a magical moment it felt like they were flying. Any fear of heights simply slipped away. Fresh air rushed at Pippa's face, lifting her dark, curly hair that was neatly held in place by a hairnet. Snowdrop cleared the wall, triumphantly flicking her tail as she landed.

'Yes!' Pippa shouted, galloping Snowdrop over the finishing line.

The crowd cheered and screamed but one voice shouted louder than the rest.

'Pippa! Are you awake? It's time to go.'

Pippa jolted out of her dream, nearly falling off her bed as Snowdrop, the showjumping arena and the cheering

7

crowds vanished. She blinked and stared round the small bedroom she shared with her big sister, Miranda.

It was easy to see which side of the room was Pippa's. Her wall was totally covered with pictures of ponies – big ones, small ones, black, brown, chestnut, roan, palomino, grey. Pippa's favourite picture of all was of Snowdrop, a silver-coloured pony with deep brown eyes.

Miranda's side used to have horse pictures too, but was now covered with posters of boys – some were famous film stars but most were in bands. Both sisters thought the other one's decor was silly.

'Are you ready, sweetheart?' Mum asked from the doorway.

'Nearly!' Pippa called, hastily jumping

off the bed and following her mum downstairs. 'Did you remember to pack my swimming costume?'

'Of course,' Mum said, smiling. 'Now off you go and get ready!'

☆

It was boiling hot and Pippa was glad that she, her mum, Miranda and their little brother, Jack, were going on holiday, swapping their terrace in the city for a cottage by the sea. Pippa was so excited she trotted up and down the pavement, riding an imaginary pony as she waited for Mum to unlock the car so that they could load the luggage into the boot.

'You're so immature,' Miranda chided, rolling her eyes as she climbed into the passenger seat.

Mum snapped Jack into his car seat and Pippa took her usual seat in the back, beside her brother.

'We're off!' cheered Pippa as Mum started the engine.

Dreamily, Pippa stared out of the window, watching the busy city streets gradually change to green fields filled with horses, cows and sheep, until, at last, they arrived at their holiday home.

'Wow! Is it all ours?' Pippa exclaimed, as Mum pulled up in front of a small, white cottage surrounded by a huge garden. 'I could have a pony if we lived here.'

'Yes, the garden's big enough!' Mum agreed, rummaging in her handbag for the key to the front door.

The cottage was right by the Pippa breathed deeply, loving the smell of the fresh, salty air.

'Can we go to the beach?' she asked.

Mum laughed at her impatience. 'Let's unpack the car first. If we're going to the beach you'll want to take your buckets and spades.'

'I'll help,' Pippa said enthusiastically, pulling her bag from the boot.

The cottage was even prettier inside than out. Pippa loved the attic bedroom, even though she had to share it with Miranda. It had sloping walls, a sea view and, to Pippa's delight, there was an old horseshoe nailed to one of the roof beams.

'Horseshoes are lucky,' she said happily.

Pippa skipped down the stairs into the kitchen, where Mum was searching their luggage for the bag containing the food.

'We'll have our lunch on the beach,' she said, packing sandwiches, cake, apples and drinks into a picnic hamper.

☆

The gate at the end of the garden opened on to a winding path that led down to the sea. Pippa was too excited to walk along it. Instead she galloped down the path, pretending to be a fiery stallion, until she reached a horseshoe-shaped cove. Pippa stared in wonder at the golden sand and sparkling blue water stretching away from her.

The cove felt so secret and special it made Pippa's insides fizz with excitement.

'It's magic,' she whispered softly.

Pulling off her sandals, she ran across the powdery sand to the sea, where tiny, white-crested waves were licking the shore. Just as Pippa was about to paddle in the water, her eyes were drawn far out to sea. What was that at the mouth of the cove?

Pippa stared in amazement at two animals splashing in the water. 'They look just like seahorses!' she gasped.

Pippa raised her arm to shield her eyes from the sun so she could take a better look. They really did look like seahorses, and they were almost as big as real horses, with gracefully curved necks bobbing above the water and long spines sticking up along a spiky mane.

One was pale pink and the other was green with dark freckles. Pippa blinked and rubbed her eyes, sure she was imagining things, but when she looked again the two animals were still there, splashing water at each other with their curled tails.

Behind her Pippa could hear Mum, Miranda and Jack laughing together as they made their way on to the beach.

'Quick!' she called, waving at them. 'Look at this!'

'What is it, darling?'

'Seahorses,' Pippa said.

'Where? I can't see them!' Jack wailed.

'Seahorses!' Miranda exclaimed. 'How can you see a tiny seahorse from here?'

'They're giant ones,' Pippa said.

'I can't see anything.' Mum stared out to sea.

Miranda giggled as she ran over. 'I see them! The red one's wearing a hat!'

Pippa's heart leapt, then sank right down to her bare toes. Miranda was teasing her! Besides, the sea was empty now. The seahorses had disappeared.

'I did see two seahorses,' Pippa insisted. 'They were playing together.'

'Don't be silly, Pip. There's no such thing as a giant seahorse,' Miranda said scornfully.

'Pippa, you're too big for that sort of make-believe,' Mum said gently. 'Come and help me set out the picnic.'

Pippa gazed at the sea but there was

nothing there except for the herring gulls gliding over the bay. But the seahorses *were* real – Pippa knew she hadn't imagined them. Full of confusion, she hurried after Mum.

'Do I have to eat now?' she asked. 'I'd like to have a paddle first.'

'Go on then,' Mum said. 'Be careful. Don't go deeper than your knees.'

Pippa ran back to the water's edge. The sea was lovely and warm. She waded out until she was knee deep. The water was so clear she could still see her feet. Pippa wiggled her toes in the sand.

'Ooooh,' she said. 'That tickles!'

Looking down, Pippa saw two tiny seahorses swimming around her feet.

'Wow! This place is full of seahorses!'

Pippa bent down for a closer look.

The moment her fingers touched the water they began to tingle. The feeling was so incredible that Pippa felt sure some kind of magic was at work. Gently, she moved her fingers to get the seahorse to swim to her hand. The tiny animal was almost there when, suddenly, with a loud *whoosh*, the sea rose up in a peak in the shape of the head and fore-legs of a galloping horse.

'Eek!' Pippa squealed.

But the wave didn't crash.

Two giant seahorses popped through the motionless wave and examined Pippa with their big eyes.

'You *are* real!' she exclaimed. 'I knew I hadn't imagined it.'

Pippa waded closer to the giant creatures and, knowing they meant her no harm, stood on her tiptoes to gently stroke their noses.

'Your name, Pippa, is short for Philippa, which means *lover of ponies*,' said the pink seahorse.

'That's right,' stuttered Pippa, who couldn't believe she was talking to a giant seahorse.

'Then you are the one,' said the green seahorse.

'My name is Rosella,' the pink seahorse continued. 'And this is Triton. We've come to take you to a place that needs your help.'

With a flick of her pink tail, Rosella scooped Pippa up, placing her gently on her back. The wave melted away and both seahorses surged forward through the foam.

'Where are we going?' Pippa asked.

'To Chevalia!'

Chapter 2

Pippa could hardly believe that she was riding a giant seahorse far out to sea. Rosella swam on, diving in and out of the waves, as Pippa clung to her gracefully arched neck. In a strange way, it was like riding a pony. Pippa stared at the delicate ears and long spines sticking out from the animal's neck.

Triton, the great, green seahorse, was swimming alongside her.

'Are you comfortable?' he asked kindly.

His voice was soft and deep, and it stopped Pippa from feeling scared. For a moment she was too speechless to answer.

'Yes, thank you,' she murmured at last. 'Are you taking me back to my mum? She'll be worrying like mad.'

Both seahorses chuckled.

'We're taking you somewhere very special, where time exists in a bubble,' explained Rosella in a gentle, feminine voice. 'You can stay there as long as you like and you won't be missed, for time will not pass in your own world.'

'Where is it?' asked Pippa, her voice quivering with excitement.

'The island of Chevalia,' said the seahorses.

Pippa looked out to the horizon and saw a large island fringed with a long, sandy beach.

'Wow!'

Pippa stared at the island in amazement. It was the most beautiful place she'd ever seen. So many questions were bubbling inside her but, before she could ask anything more, Rosella tipped her into the water and nudged her gently ashore.

'Chevalia is in danger but you can help save it,' said Rosella.

'Me? But how?'

'That is your quest,' said Triton.

'Good luck, Pippa, lover of ponies,' called Rosella.

She dived under the water with Triton and they swam away.

Pippa scrambled to her feet. She was standing on a sandy beach edged with leafy, green trees. At first it was very quiet. The only sound was the soft hiss of the sea gently lapping the shore.

Suddenly she heard a low drumming. Squinting into the sun, she saw a pony galloping towards her along the beach.

Its long tail streamed out like a banner and golden sand sprayed up from its hooves. Pippa's heart was racing. Who was this coming to meet her?

With a snort of surprise, the pony pulled up, sliding to a stop a short way from Pippa. It was pure white and wore a tiara studded with sparkling, pink diamonds. The pony's dark brown eyes shone with excitement.

'A girl!' Reaching out, the pony touched Pippa with a velvety nose. 'A real, live girl!'

Pippa stared back.

'Y-you . . . you can talk?' she stuttered. Pippa couldn't take her eyes off her. She was the most beautiful pony she'd ever seen.

'Of course,' said the pony, tossing her head. 'All ponies can talk, but only special humans can hear us. I'm Princess Stardust, seventh foal of the Queen and King of Chevalia. What's your name?'

'Pippa,' she answered. 'I'm the . . . second child . . . of the MacDonald family . . . of Burlington Terrace.'

'Have you been sent to help us?' Stardust's voice trembled.

'Help you?' repeated Pippa.

'To find the missing horseshoes,' said Stardust impatiently. 'If the eight magical horseshoes aren't found and returned to the Whispering Wall in time for sundown on Midsummer Day, then Chevalia will be lost for ever. Quick! Jump on my back. I'll take you to the Castle to meet my mother and father.'

Excitement and fear fizzled through Pippa. She was on a secret island with talking ponies and she was going to meet the Queen and King! She'd only ridden a few times – and never bare-back. But here in Chevalia, anything seemed possible. Pushing aside her

fears, she swiftly vaulted on to Stardust's back.

'Hold on to my mane!' called Stardust.

As Pippa sank her hands into Stardust's silky mane, the pony spun round
and galloped across the beach towards
the trees.

'We'll cut through the Wild Forest,'

Stardust neighed. 'It's out of bounds but it's the quickest way home.'

Pippa caught a glimpse of eight tall turrets rising above the treetops. The turrets disappeared as Stardust entered the Wild Forest. Pippa shivered as the dark woods swallowed them too.

Chapter 3

There were lots of ponies in the forest, all with tangled manes and dirty coats. They were playing chasing games and having such fun Pippa almost wished that there was time to stop and meet them. But Stardust thundered on, dodging bramble bushes and jumping over fallen trees. Pippa sat firmly, gripping with her knees and ducking to avoid the low-hanging branches. The

Wild Forest was on the side of a hill and, as it grew steeper, Stardust slowed. She was breathing noisily and her sides were heaving.

'Stardust, stop and let me walk,' Pippa called out, concerned.

'It's too dangerous for you,' panted Stardust. 'The forest is filled with quick-stick mud that would swallow you whole.'

Pippa gulped. She didn't like the idea of being eaten by mud.

'But don't worry,' added Stardust. 'I know the way!'

A little while later, the woods began to thin. Stardust sped up as they broke through the trees and came out on the edge of a large, grassy plateau. On the opposite side to the Wild Forest was a range of hills. To the right, at the other end of the plain, Pippa saw a wide road, a collection of buildings and a Sand School, where a group of ponies was gathered. Stardust started to gallop across the plain towards the hills when one of the ponies, waddling on stubby legs, noticed her.

'Princess Stardust! Come here at once!' she bellowed out.

Stardust pretended not to hear, until the pony broke away from the group and galloped after them.

'Oh, horseflies!' Stardust exclaimed, pulling up and waiting.

'Who is it?' Pippa asked curiously, as the stocky, brown pony hurried towards them.

Stardust rolled her eyes. 'Mrs Steeple-chase, our nanny. She's just taken my brothers and sisters to school. I should be there too.'

Mrs Steeplechase stopped in front of Stardust, her nostrils flaring angrily.

'What do you think you are doing? The Wild Forest is *strictly* out of bounds.'

'Sorry,' Stardust apologised. 'I thought school had been cancelled because of the emergency. I was looking for the missing horseshoes but instead I found Pippa. She's been sent to help us. Isn't that fantastic?'

Suddenly Mrs Steeplechase noticed Pippa.

'A human girl!' she snorted with alarm. 'And what's she doing riding on your back as if you were just any old pony? Get down, girl. You can walk the rest of the way.'

'But –' said Stardust.

'Don't argue,' said Mrs Steeplechase fiercely. 'She might be dangerous. I dread to think what Queen Moonshine and King Firestar will say about this. A girl indeed!'

Pippa's heart sank. She hoped that the King and Queen weren't as unfriendly as the royal nanny. Pink with embarrassment, she slid down from Stardust's back.

'Don't mind Mrs Steeplechase — she's all whinny and no kick. Mum and Dad will be thrilled to see you,' Stardust whispered reassuringly. She began to mimic Mrs Steeplechase, walking stiffly after her, copying the way Mrs Steeplechase's large bottom was swinging from side to side.

Giggling quietly, Pippa followed Stardust over the Plateau and along a winding path. After a while, the path opened out at the top of a hill. Pippa stopped and stared.

Ahead of her, nestling among the other hills, was Stableside Castle, the biggest castle she'd ever seen. Its white stone walls sparkled like pearls in the bright sunlight. Eight flags, each a different colour but all decorated with a golden horseshoe, fluttered from the tall turrets, and the enormous wooden drawbridge was lowered, as if to welcome them.

'That's my turret,' Stardust said, pointing her nose at the smallest one, which was topped by a pink flag, waving in the breeze. 'It's got the best view in the whole castle.'

A group of horses was clustered around the drawbridge with cameras slung round their necks, obviously waiting for someone to arrive or leave.

Mrs Steeplechase tutted. 'The ponarazzi are still here then! We'll have to take the secret path and go in through the back way or else the girl's picture will be all over the island by tomorrow.'

'They're always trying to take pictures of the Royal Family,' said Stardust.

'No talking and hurry up,' Mrs Steeplechase said sternly, as she trotted down the hill towards a small door concealed in the Castle's walls.

Pippa's stomach churned uncomfortably as she followed behind Mrs Steeplechase. Stardust's hooves crunched on the white gravel at the base of the Castle wall, and Mrs Steeplechase turned to Stardust.

'Try to trot quietly, child,' she said.

But Stardust took no notice of the rotund nanny and continued to clatter beside her, not seeming at all worried that she was in trouble.

The hidden door led into a large courtyard with a stage on one side, backed by a huge, stone wall. The wall was bare except for eight iron nails sticking out of it forlornly. Stardust blinked back a tear.

'That's where the golden horseshoes should hang,' she whispered.

A wave of sadness hit Pippa and she had to catch her breath. She glanced around and saw piles of silk ribbons, rosettes and flowers strewn across the ground. It was as if the courtyard had

been abandoned suddenly. A small, chestnut pony was sweeping them up. A trail
of black hoof marks led to the door they'd
entered by. Pippa stared at the marks.
Something about them bothered her but
she couldn't quite put her finger on it.

'We were decorating the Castle for
the Midsummer Ball,' Stardust said,
nodding at the ribbons. 'But now no
one has the heart to get things ready.
It's only a week away and it takes ages
to prepare everything, especially the
food for the banquet.'

Mrs Steeplechase trotted across the
courtyard to a wooden door guarded
by a black pony wearing a red sash.
Grandly, the pony bowed his head, then
nudged open the door.

'This is the Royal Court,' Stardust whispered, as they entered a large room full of perfectly groomed ponies with gleaming coats and polished hooves.

One by one they fell silent, staring at Pippa with wide eyes as she walked across the room. Pippa felt very small as she made her way nervously through

the crowd. All of the ponies wore brightly coloured sashes and some were decorated with jewels. A chestnut pony, with bulging eyes, a square nose and emeralds in her mane, gave Pippa a particularly mean look. Next to her, a smaller pony, with the same shaped nose and eyes, gave her an identical, hard stare.

'That's Baroness Divine and her daughter Cinders,' whispered Stardust. 'No one likes them. They think they're so much better than anyone else. Cinders shouldn't even be here. She should be at school, like me.'

Mrs Steeplechase stopped in front of a beautiful palomino pony with a long, white mane and tail, and her companion, a large, copper-coloured pony. Stiffly, she bent one leg, bowing her head to the ground. Stardust copied, leaving Pippa standing awkwardly between them. Unsure what to do, Pippa curtsied as if she were greeting her ballet teacher.

'Your Majesties,' said Mrs Steeplechase, rising slowly. 'Princess Stardust has found a stranger on our island. A human.'

'So I can see,' said the Queen, her brown eyes resting on Pippa. 'What is your name, child? And where do you come from?'

Overcome with shyness, Pippa stuttered her name.

'P-P-Pippa MacDonald. From Burlington Terrace.'

'Isn't it brilliant!' said Stardust.
'Pippa's been sent to help us find the
missing horseshoes.'

A surprised murmur rippled round
the room. Baroness Divine stepped
forward.

'No human has ever set foot on
Chevalia before. How can we trust her?'
she demanded shrilly.

'She's a pony lover,' said Stardust
indignantly. 'Only a true pony lover can
find Chevalia and understand our
language.'

Queen Moonshine stared at Pippa,
making her squirm inside, but she stood
tall, hoping the Queen would see that
she had nothing to hide.

'Chevalia is a very special place. It

relies on horse and pony lovers from around the world to keep it alive,' the Queen said in a low voice. 'Their love is captured by the eight magical horseshoes that hang on the Whispering Wall. Once a year, the magic in those horseshoes must be renewed by the Midsummer sun or it will fade. If that happens, then our beautiful island will sink into the sea.'

Pippa gulped. Now she understood why Princess Stardust was so sad that the wall was bare.

'This is a time of grave crisis,' Baroness Divine continued. 'Midsummer Day will soon be upon us but the magical horseshoes have disappeared. How did you get here? Who told you that Chevalia needed help? How do we know we can trust you?'

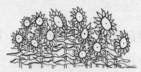

Chapter 4

The Royal Court was so silent that Pippa was sure everyone would hear her heart thudding.

'I didn't know Chevalia needed my help,' she answered truthfully. 'I was on holiday with my family when a magic wave scooped me up. Rosella and Triton rescued me and they brought me here.'

The ponies stared at Pippa in awe.

An excited murmur rippled around the regal room.

'The human girl saw Rosella and Triton – but why? They never show themselves to humans.'

The Queen stamped a hoof for silence.

'There is an old legend that tells of a human girl who comes to Chevalia in its time of need. The seahorses brought you here, so I believe you are that girl.' She touched Pippa on the top of her head with her muzzle. 'Welcome to Chevalia. Good luck with your quest. If there is anything you need, then please ask.'

'She needs me,' Stardust said, trotting forward.

Mrs Steeplechase frowned.

'Hush,' she chided. 'You may only speak to the Queen when she speaks to you.'

'But Pippa is *my* pet! I found her. Besides, how else will she find her way around the island?' Stardust insisted.

The Queen smothered a smile.

'I'm sure we can find Pippa a good guide,' she answered. 'Perhaps your big sister Crystal —'

'I'd really like Stardust to help me,' Pippa said bravely, interrupting the Queen.

The Queen looked uncertain.

'Let Stardust help,' the King said. 'It will be good for her to have some responsibility for a change.'

'Very well,' said the Queen. 'You'd better start straight away. Time is running out.'

'Thanks, Mum,' whinnied Stardust. 'Your Majesty,' she added hastily, when Mrs Steeplechase glared at her.

As Stardust and Pippa left the Court, Cinders started complaining.

'It's not fair,' she whispered loudly, so that Pippa could hear. 'Princess Stardust gets everything. I want a girl too. I've wanted one much longer than she has.'

'Hush,' said the Baroness. 'Better things come to those who wait.'

'What does she mean?' asked Pippa.

'Don't pay any attention to her — she's always been jealous of the Royal Family,' said Stardust. 'Come on. Let's start searching for the missing horse-shoes.'

Stardust used the same hidden door they'd entered the Castle by.

'Where are we going first?' asked Pippa.

'Mane Street,' said Stardust. 'It's where everyone hangs out.'

'It doesn't sound like a very good hiding place,' Pippa said doubtfully.

'Exactly!' said Stardust. 'If I were hiding something that's where I'd put it because no one would think to look there. Hop on my back. It's so much fun when we gallop together.'

'But what about Mrs Steeplechase?' asked Pippa.

'Horseflies to Mrs Steeplechase!

Mum and Dad didn't tell you not to ride me, did they?'

Pippa didn't need a second invitation. She loved riding Stardust and her mouth stretched into a wide grin as she vaulted on to her back.

☆

Mane Street was the wide, grassy road on the Plateau that they had crossed earlier.

'That's my school,' Stardust said proudly, as they passed by Canter's Prep School for Fine Equine. 'Miss Huckleby is the best teacher ever. You should hear her read *Black Beauty*.'

Stardust's school was a blue, wooden building with window boxes overflowing with colourful flowers and tubs filled with carrot sprouts.

'The carrots are for snacking on,' Stardust said, pulling up two and giving one to Pippa.

Crunching on their carrots, they peered in through the windows, where a class of ponies was starting a maths lesson.

Stardust giggled.

'Look at Honey admiring her sparkly

hoof polish. She's my third big sister. The grumpy-looking pony wearing the boring wooden tiara with the acorns is Cloud, my second big sister. My eldest sister is Crystal. She's left Canter's now. She's going to be Queen one day and she never lets us forget it!'

Cloud turned to the window with a scowl, and Stardust quickly pulled Pippa away.

'Don't let her see you,' she said. 'She'd want to know why I'm not in school and there isn't time to explain.'

They crept round the back of the school, passing the Sand School Pippa had seen earlier, and a green field where some tiny ponies were learning to trot. Stardust barely glanced their way, but Pippa held back, sure she saw something glinting in the long grass at the edge of the field. Could it be one of the missing horseshoes? She hurried over and was disappointed to find it was just an ordinary old horseshoe.

Pippa's eyes grew wider and wider as Stardust pranced along Mane Street pointing out all of her favourite shops. Pippa noticed that all the shoppers were looking at her too!

'That's the salon where I go to have my mane and tail washed. They have gorgeous strawberry-scented shampoo. And look – Dolly's Tea Rooms. You should taste their buckets of hot carrot juice. Delicious!' Stardust said, smacking her lips. 'And there's Mr Gems. He sells the nicest jewels ever.'

It reminded her of the high street back at home, only Mane Street was much prettier, with beds of sunflowers decorating the pavements and tiny silver horseshoes strung from the old-fashioned street lamps. Everywhere was spotlessly clean – even the silver water troughs had been polished until they shone. The street was packed with ponies and Pippa was amazed to see so many different types. There were well-groomed ponies, stocky working ones and scruffy little Shetlands. Everyone seemed very quiet, mostly talking in whispers. When a pony whinnied with laughter, it earned them a glare.

'It's been like this since the horse-shoes went missing,' sighed Stardust.

Pippa was beginning to doubt that they'd find any of the golden horseshoes here. There were too many ponies and not enough hiding places. There was a funfair at the end of the street, though. That looked like a more promising place to hide things.

'Shall we try in there?' she asked.

'That's where I'm taking you!' Stardust said excitedly. 'You should see the merry-go-round. It's rainbow-coloured with tiny flashing lights. It's so pretty. And the ghost train is really scary. It's even got Night Mares.'

'Night Mares?' asked Pippa. 'What do you mean?'

'The Night Mares are spooky-looking ponies. They've lived here for

ever, even when Chevalia was just a tiny lump of volcanic rock and not the magical island it is today. I've never seen one but everyone says they're really mean.' Stardust shivered. 'Do you want a ride on the ghost train? It's great fun.'

'I thought we were looking for the horseshoes,' said Pippa.

Stardust went pink.

'We are! It's just so brilliant having you here and I want to show you everything. But you're right. Finding the horseshoes is the most important thing. Without them Chevalia will lose its magic.'

Stardust shuddered, her brown eyes suddenly glistening with tears.

'Don't worry,' Pippa said, stroking her neck. 'I promise we'll find the horseshoes.'

'Really?' sniffed Stardust. 'Thank you, Pippa. You're the best pet ever.'

Pippa opened her mouth to argue that she wasn't a pet, but Stardust was already heading into the fair.

The fair was less crowded than Mane Street. None of the ponies, except for the really young ones, seemed to be enjoying themselves. Pippa and Stardust walked around the rides but found nothing.

'Let's search the rest of the Plateau,' Stardust said eventually. 'It's big enough to hide all eight of the horseshoes.'

☆

Pippa and Stardust spent the rest of the day walking the Plateau. It was hard work and there were many false alarms. By teatime Pippa had met many of Stardust's friends and they had both found lots of precious items that other young ponies had lost, like hairclips and combs, but they hadn't found any of the golden horseshoes.

As the sun began to set, they made their way back to the Castle. Pippa was hungry and very frustrated that they

hadn't discovered anything about where the missing horseshoes might be.

'We both need a hoof massage with dandelion hoof balm,' Stardust said longingly, as they passed by the Mane Street Salon. 'But Mrs Steeplechase is very strict about mealtimes. She won't let us go out together tomorrow if we're late.'

'We *must* find those magical horse-shoes tomorrow,' said Pippa.

☆

Meals were eaten in a huge dining room with three stone feeding troughs, and a special gold one at the top of the room for the Queen and King. Once again, everyone stared at Pippa as she followed Stardust to a trough.

As the serving ponies carried in buckets of steaming oats and carrot mash, Pippa wondered what she was going to eat, but she needn't have worried. One of the cooks came out of the kitchen to serve her personally.

'Fish and chips!' Pippa cried delight-edly. 'My favourite food!'

There was even a knife and fork to

eat it with. As Pippa tucked in hungrily, Stardust watched in amazement.

'So that's what those are for!' she exclaimed. 'I've only ever seen them in the Museum of Human Artefacts.'

Pippa laughed and listened to the ponies whinnying around her. Most of their chatter was about the missing horseshoes. Pippa caught her own name several times and a few of the ponies shyly nodded at her. But not everyone was as friendly. Several refused to look, turning away if Pippa smiled at them. She finished her meal with a rosy red apple and felt better for having eaten after such an eventful day.

When Stardust and Pippa left the dining room to go to bed, one pony neighed at them as they passed.

'It's funny how the girl arrived at the same time that the horseshoes disappeared. I don't trust her.'

The words stung, but Pippa held her head up high. The ponies of Chevalia needed her and she wasn't going to let them down.

Chapter 5

Stardust's room was right at the top of the eighth tower of the Castle, reached by a spiral ramp. It was large and round, with curved stone walls. On her dressing table, in pride of place, was a little doll that had washed up on shore.

'I've wanted a girl ever since I was a foal but I never dreamt I'd get one,' Stardust explained.

'I've wanted a pony for ever too,' said Pippa.

Stardust looked confused but then she laughed.

'I get it! You're my pet and I'm yours.'

'Can't we just be friends?' Pippa asked.

'Friends,' Stardust said slowly. 'That sounds nice. Yes, let's be friends.'

'You're a magical friend,' said Pippa.

'No, you're a magical friend.' Stardust laughed.

Stardust slept in a huge bed with a straw duvet and a horseshoe-shaped headboard covered with rosettes. Pippa slept on a special put-you-up next to her. The bed was surprisingly comfortable and she fell asleep immediately.

☆

The next morning, Pippa woke early.
Stardust was still snoring softly, so
she stared out of the window. Pippa
was terrified of heights and at first it
made her feel queasy being so high
up. Taking deep breaths, she looked
out over the magical island. It calmed
her down to think about all of these
ponies living together in such a special
place. She gazed down on the Plateau
to see ponies strolling on Mane Street
and in the distance she spotted ponies
working the fields in the Grasslands.
As she looked out to the sea, she could
see nothing around for miles, and she
reminded herself that Chevalia
would be lost if she didn't keep her
promise.

Pippa counted the days on her fingers. There were only six left until Midsummer. Time was running out. They had to find the golden horseshoes before it was too late. Yesterday had been fun but Pippa worried that Stardust had been more enthusiastic about touring Chevalia and showing off her new friend than she had been about searching for the missing horseshoes. But today would be different. Pippa decided it was time to take charge.

Anxious to get started, Pippa gently shook her new friend awake.

'You're still here!' Stardust whinnied with delight as she opened her eyes. 'I thought I might have dreamt you.'

Quickly, she rolled out of bed and nuzzled Pippa's dark hair.

'Me too,' said Pippa. 'But it's not a dream and we're going to find the missing horseshoes.'

Stardust took ages getting ready so Pippa helped, combing her long mane and tail, to hurry her along.

'I've been wondering where to go today,' Stardust said idly. 'We could visit the Grasslands or the beaches. Or perhaps we should start with the Savannah where the striped ponies roam wild. Then there's the Horseshoe Hills and the Volcano. Maybe not the Volcano – it's spooky there.' Stardust shivered.

Pippa stopped combing as something clicked into place.

'The Volcano!' she exclaimed. 'Maybe that would explain the black hoof marks I saw in the courtyard yesterday. I wondered where they'd come from. Everywhere in Chevalia seems so clean, especially around the Castle, but volcanoes are covered in ash.'

'Are you sure?' Stardust asked

uncertainly. 'Wouldn't you rather search the beaches? We might find some clues there.'

'But the black hoof marks are a clue!' Pippa said, her voice rising with excitement. 'We *have* to search the Volcano.'

'I'm not sure,' Stardust said reluctantly. 'Storm – he's my youngest brother – told me never to go there. It's too dangerous.'

'Then I'll go on my own,' Pippa said stubbornly.

Stardust's eyes widened.

'You'd really do that?'

Pippa nodded. She'd promised to save Chevalia and she meant to keep her word, no matter how dangerous it was.

'Then I'm coming with you,' said Stardust.

Pippa hugged Stardust round the neck, pleased that she didn't have to go to the Volcano alone.

Even though she was nervous, Pippa was impatient to get started. After a hurried breakfast of cereal and apples, she and Stardust left the Castle by a back entrance. It was very early and the door was still locked. Stardust drew back the bolts with her teeth.

'Maybe the Night Mares stole our horseshoes,' wondered Stardust. 'Storm thinks that they live on the Volcano, but Comet, my bookworm brother, says that's just a myth. But if it was the Night Mares then how did they get inside the

Castle? All the doors are locked from the inside at night.'

'Perhaps someone helped them,' suggested Pippa.

'No!' Stardust exclaimed, sounding shocked. 'Why would anyone do that?'

Pippa shrugged. She didn't know either. Chevalia was so special, she couldn't imagine anyone wanting to harm it.

Pippa could hardly believe how much her riding had improved in such a short time. She felt as comfortable riding Stardust bareback as if she'd been riding with a saddle. How impressed her pony-mad friends back home would be if they could see her now!

At last, they entered the Foothills,

keeping to the path so that they didn't get lost. The higher they went, the steeper the path grew. Sometimes it ran alongside the cliff face. Pippa didn't like that – it made her dizzy to look down and see the jagged rocks falling away beneath her. Stardust seemed to sense her fear and kept away from the edge.

It was very peaceful. The only sounds were the clopping of Stardust's hooves, the cry of the birds soaring overhead, and a soft rushing noise that Pippa couldn't work out until they reached a small stream that crossed the path.

'So that's what I could hear,' Pippa said, as Stardust jumped the stream then stopped for a drink.

'Try some,' she said. 'It's fresh and it's clean.'

Pippa slid from Stardust's back and, kneeling down, scooped up the water in cupped hands. It was freezing cold and made her fingers tingle.

'Mmm, that's delicious,' she said, enjoying a long drink.

Stardust nudged her playfully, her long, white mane falling over Pippa's arm.

'That tickles!' Pippa giggled, nudging Stardust back.

Stardust dipped a hoof in the stream, splashing water at Pippa.

'Water fight!' she neighed.

'Water fight!' Pippa agreed enthusiastically, splashing Stardust back.

Stardust splashed with her hooves and Pippa with her feet. They disappeared in a shower of water, which sparkled like diamonds in the sunshine, until Pippa and Stardust were soaking wet.

'Stop!' Pippa begged, pushing her soggy curls away from her face.

'That was such fun,' Stardust

whinnied, shaking herself dry and soaking Pippa all over again.

'Eeww!' squealed Pippa. 'I didn't think I could get any wetter!'

It was already very hot, and as the friends climbed higher the sun soon dried Pippa's clothes. After a while, they followed another stream that snaked alongside the path before tumbling over a cliff in a fast-flowing waterfall.

'It's beautiful!' gasped Pippa.

'Chevalia is beautiful,' Stardust said, her face clouding with worry. 'I can't understand why the Night Mares would want to harm it.'

'It might not have been them,' said Pippa.

'Who else could it have been?' asked Stardust. 'No one knows about Chevalia. Only true pony lovers can see it and a true pony lover would never harm us.'

Pippa twisted a curl of her hair around her finger. 'But the island's not going to disappear. We're going to find the golden horseshoes.'

'Promise?' asked Stardust.

'Yes,' said Pippa.

Knowing it was a sign of friendship in ponies, she leaned forward, softly blowing air at Stardust's nostrils.

Stardust blew air back.

'Thank you, Pippa,' she whispered. 'You're a true friend.'

Pippa fought back her worries as she

smiled at Stardust. Promises were easy to make, but could she really keep hers?

Yes, she told herself firmly. She would not break her word. She *would* find the golden horseshoes in time to save Chevalia.

Chapter 6

As Pippa and Stardust neared the base of the Volcano, the path grew steeper and it was strewn with black rocks.

'They're hot!' exclaimed Pippa. She picked one up and quickly put it down again, brushing the black dirt from her hands.

'Yes, and this is as far as we can go,' Stardust said nervously. 'I think the Night Mares live near here.'

'So now we look for clues?' Pippa asked.

Stardust nodded.

'But only on this side of the Volcano. We mustn't stray into the Cloud Forest on the other side. No one's allowed to go there. Not even Mum and Dad.'

'Why not?' asked Pippa.

'It's haunted,' she whispered.

'Oh,' Pippa said, feeling both scared and relieved.

The Volcano was so big it would have taken for ever if they'd had to search it all. On the other hand, she hoped she wouldn't have to look for the horse-shoes in a haunted forest.

Side by side, Pippa and Stardust started to hunt for clues. At first

Pippa was very excited, thinking that they might find all eight of the horse-shoes. The rocky landscape had lots of nooks and crannies, perfect for hiding things in. Each time she saw something glinting in the sun Pippa rushed forward, and each time she was disappointed.

'I'm thirsty,' Stardust said at last. Her white coat was smudged with dirt and her long tail was full of tangles. 'Let's go back to the stream for a drink.'

She was trotting towards the path when something soared overhead.

'What's that?' Pippa cried, pointing upwards.

Stardust swung round.

'What?' she asked. 'I can't see anything.'

'It's gone.' Pippa was dismayed.

'Maybe it was an eagle?' said Stardust.

Pippa fell silent. The thing she'd seen had been far too big to be an eagle but, as she followed Stardust to the stream, the creature flew over again. Pippa's eyes widened.

'Look!' she shouted. 'It's a flying horse!'

Stardust spun round again.

'Peggy!' she exclaimed.

Peggy had a silvery coat, a long mane and tail, and an enormous pair of feathery wings. She circled overhead, tilting slightly as she drifted through the air.

'She's amazing,' Pippa breathed, her

heart thudding. 'Stardust, I think she's trying to tell us something!'

'I don't think so,' said Stardust. 'Peggy hardly ever shows herself — you're honoured to have seen her. I think she's curious about you.'

Pippa shielded her eyes with her hands as she squinted at the flying horse.

'But look how she keeps dipping her wing. It's at the same place every time. And then she turns her head to see if we're watching her.'

Stardust watched in silence.

'It might be just a coincidence, but perhaps we should check it out,' she said at last.

Forgetting their thirst, Pippa and Stardust hurried back the way they'd come. Peggy remained overhead, still flying in the same circle, until the friends were directly underneath her. Suddenly she swooped much lower, hovering right above a rocky ledge. Whinnying loudly, she reared up. Then, with a flick of her silvery tail, she flew away.

'Look!' Pippa said, breaking into a run. 'There's something sparkly up there on the ledge.'

Pippa and Stardust raced across the rocks until they reached the ledge that Peggy had showed them.

Stardust neighed with excitement.

'I can see something shining in the grass.'

Pippa stood on tiptoes. In the middle

of a scrubby clump of grass, something was shining with a soft, yellow glow.

'It must be one of our golden horse-shoes!' she exclaimed.

The horseshoe was so well hidden that if it hadn't been for Peggy, Pippa and Stardust would never have spotted it. Nervously, Pippa rubbed her hands on her shorts. The ledge was over twice her height and she'd have to climb it to reach the horseshoe. The thought made her feel hot and shaky. She couldn't do it. The ledge was far too high.

'Stand on my back,' Stardust said eagerly.

Pippa hesitated, for she had always been nervous of heights.

'Don't worry – you won't hurt me. I'm

really strong,' Stardust said, misunderstanding Pippa's concern.

Reluctantly, Pippa vaulted on to Stardust's back, sitting for a moment to work up the courage to go on.

Come on, you can do this, she silently urged herself.

Slowly, Pippa stood up. Her heart

was racing and her legs trembled like a jellyfish. Stardust remained completely still and, gradually, Pippa relaxed. That wasn't so bad! Now all she had to do was stretch up to retrieve the missing horseshoe. But, frustratingly, it was just out of reach. Pippa stretched as far as she dared – any further and she'd lose her balance.

'It's no good,' she called at last. 'I can't get it. Can you move any closer?'

'I'm as close as I can get,' said Stardust.

Pippa stared at the ground and immediately wished she hadn't. Quickly, she sat back down, clinging on to Stardust's mane until her head had stopped swimming.

'Are you OK?' asked Stardust.

'I'm fine,' Pippa replied, licking her dry lips.

She was going to have to dismount and climb up to the ledge instead. But as she slid down from Stardust's back, she saw a long, sturdy stick. Snatching it up, she waved it in relief.

'I might be able to reach the horse-shoe with this.'

Taking great care not to hit Stardust with the stick, Pippa scrambled on to her back once more. But as she reached up to hook the horseshoe, she froze. What was that? Above the ledge, to the right, was a large slab of rock where two scruffy-looking ponies, with thin, straggly manes and tails, were arguing loudly. Pippa's insides turned to ice.

'They must be Night Mares!' she whispered.

Chapter 7

Hardly daring to breathe, Pippa listened to the Night Mares' argument.

'How did you manage to drop a horseshoe, Nightshade?' the smaller pony whinnied crossly. 'The Mistress said to hide it carefully so that the Royal Ponies wouldn't find it! It just goes to show that even though you're bigger than me, you're not smarter.'

'Be quiet, Eclipse. Nagging me isn't

going to help me get the horseshoe back,' Nightshade whinnied.

'But how will we reach it from here?'

'Use that branch behind you.'

As Eclipse turned to examine the branch, Pippa snapped into action. With trembling hands, she reached up to hook the golden horseshoe down from the ledge. It was very heavy and, although Pippa's stick was long enough to touch it, she couldn't drag the horse-shoe towards her. Swallowing her frustration, she tried again.

'What's happening?' called Stardust. 'Have you got it yet?'

'Ssssh,' whispered Pippa.

But it was too late.

'Who's that?' asked Nightshade. She

peered over the outcrop of rock and
her eyes locked with Pippa's. 'Eclipse,
it's a girl!' she neighed. 'And she's steal-
ing my horseshoe!'

'Prancing ponies!' cursed Eclipse.

Breathing heavily, Pippa blotted
out Nightshade and Eclipse's frantic

conversation and concentrated on getting the horseshoe. Using both hands to hold the stick, and hoping that Stardust wouldn't move a muscle, she dragged the horseshoe down. But Eclipse had also found a stick on the ground and tried to pull the horseshoe up. It was turning into a tug of war! Luckily, despite Eclipse's stick being larger than Pippa's, the pony was holding it in her mouth and having difficulty controlling it. Steadily, Pippa dragged the horseshoe to the edge of the ledge. As she reached out to pick it up, Eclipse brought her stick crashing down.

Just in time, Pippa snatched her hand out of the way. She sat down on Stardust's back and tightly clutched the horseshoe.

'I've got it!' she said triumphantly.

'Hold on tight!' Stardust said, turning sharply to gallop back down the Volcano.

'That's *my* horseshoe!' Nightshade shouted after her.

As Stardust gathered speed, her hooves thumping on the ash-covered path, the Night Mares' voices faded away.

Pippa started to wonder who Eclipse had meant by 'the Mistress'. She clung on to Stardust, wrapping her free hand around the white mane and gripping with her knees. Stardust didn't stop until she was safely at the bottom of the Volcano, where she pulled up under the shade of a tree. Pippa slid down from her back and fanned her friend with a feathery, green leaf. It was several minutes before Stardust got her breath back.

'We did it,' Stardust said, trembling with excitement. 'We found our first horseshoe. I can't wait to show Mum and Dad. They'll be thrilled!'

Pippa's smile was so wide it almost reached her ears, but her stomach churned nervously. That had been so scary.

'So you were right – it *was* the Night Mares who stole the horseshoes!'

She hoped the other seven horse-shoes would be easier to retrieve, but what if they couldn't find them?

'What do you think?' Stardust asked impatiently, pawing the ground with a hoof.

'Sorry, what did you say?' Pippa real-ised that she hadn't been listening.

'Nightshade and Eclipse think we've gone home,' Stardust repeated. 'We could sneak back and follow them. They might let slip where the other horseshoes are – or who this mysterious Mistress is.'

Pippa slid the golden horseshoe into her pocket.

'I think we should take this one back to the Castle first and hang it where it belongs. We don't want to lose it again.'

Stardust sighed. Her new friend was very sensible.

'You're right. The horseshoe needs to be back on the wall so that it can pick up the love from all the horse and pony lovers around the world. It's what keeps Chevalia alive.'

In silence, they hurried back to the Castle, entering by the back door and going straight to the Royal Court.

As the guard opened the large

wooden door, Pippa pulled the horse-shoe from her pocket and handed it to Stardust.

'You take this,' she said.

'No way!' exclaimed Stardust. 'You rescued it. You can give it to Mum and Dad.'

The Royal Court was packed and noisy, but when the ponies saw the golden horseshoe they immediately fell silent. Self-consciously, Pippa followed Stardust over to her parents.

Queen Moonshine's eyes lit up with joy.

'You've found one of our horse-shoes!' she whinnied. 'That's wonderful. I'm so proud of you both.'

'This is fantastic,' King Firestar

agreed, stamping a large hoof. 'And now the horseshoe must be put back where it belongs.'

One of the Court's helpers trotted over, but the King waved him away.

'Thank you, Conker, but I shall hang the horseshoe myself,' he said.

Pippa was pleased – she didn't really want to hand over the missing horse-shoe to anyone other than the Queen or the King.

A procession of horses followed them to the Whispering Wall, where King Firestar rehung the horseshoe. Stardust was so excited that she couldn't stand still and she danced on the spot.

When the horseshoe was back in its place, the crowd neighed loudly. But the single horseshoe looked very small and lonely hanging on the wall.

Pippa clapped, but part of her felt anxious. There was still so much to do.

'Congratulations,' Queen Moonshine said in a low voice. 'But your quest has only just begun. Midsummer Day will soon be here and there are still seven horseshoes to find. Go safely, my children, and remember not to count your horseshoes until they're hung!'

'We won't, Your Majesty,' Pippa said earnestly.

Both the Queen's words and seeing the golden horseshoe hanging on the wall had filled her with a new confidence. They could do this. Together she and Stardust would find all of the missing horseshoes.

'To Chevalia!' she cheered.

'To Chevalia!' Stardust echoed. 'And to you, Pippa, my magical friend!'

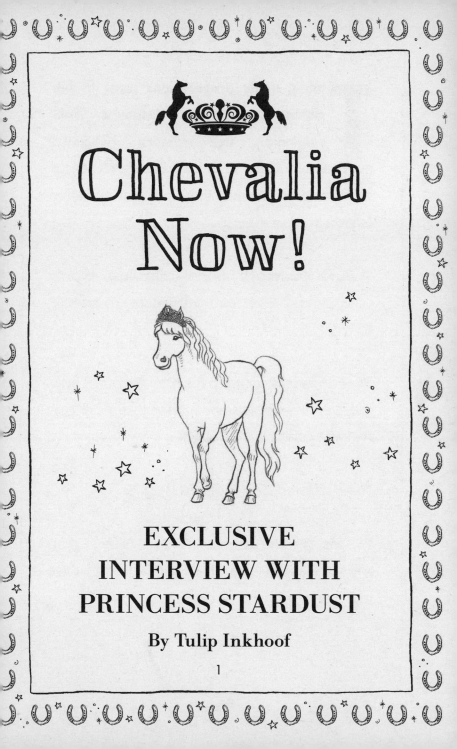

Chevalia Now!

EXCLUSIVE INTERVIEW WITH PRINCESS STARDUST

By Tulip Inkhoof

Today, while preparations were in full swing for the big Midsummer Ball, something extraordinary happened on Chevalia. Reporter Tulip Inkhoof catches up with Princess Stardust in a rare and exclusive interview.

☆ **TI (Tulip Inkhoof):** Princess Stardust, thank you so much for taking the time to speak to me.

☆ **PS (Princess Stardust):** It's my pleasure. But, please, no photos until after I've had my mane combed.

☆ **TI:** Of course. So, shall we begin?

☆ **PS:** Yes, and I must say, it's very nice to put my hooves up after the whirlwind day I've just had.

2

☆ **TI:** Yes, please tell our readers about it.

☆ **PS:** Well, I was off for a morning trot along the beach, where I like to look for seashells, when I suddenly saw a real, live girl. She had a dark, curly mane and she was just standing on our beach!

☆ **TI:** Were you scared?

☆ **PS:** I thought I was still dreaming! You see, I've always wanted a little girl for a pet.

Her name is Pippa MacDonald and she's the best pet a Princess Pony could have – oops, I mean, best friend.

☆ **TI:** Where did Pippa come from?

☆ **PS:** She came from somewhere called Burlington Terrace. It must be a very strange place indeed because Pippa says they have ponies for pets there! Can you imagine? Ponies as pets! She says the funniest things.

☆ **TI:** And why is she here?

☆ **PS:** Pippa was brought here by the seahorses Triton and Rosella, to help us find the missing magical horseshoes.

☆ **TI:** So the rumours are true – the horseshoes are missing?

☆ **PS:** Oh dear, have I put my hoof in my mouth? I shouldn't have said that.

☆ **TI:** No, no. Please go on . . .

☆ **PS:** Well, early this morning, when Mum and Dad woke up, they discovered that the eight magical horseshoes were no longer on the Whispering Wall.

☆ **TI:** But those horseshoes are very old and very precious, aren't they?

☆ **PS:** Oh yes, but they're more than just

precious – they're magical! Every year they catch the energy of the Midsummer sun and that's what keeps Chevalia from fading away.

☆ **TI:** Now I'm scared.

☆ **PS:** Oh, there's no need. You see, Pippa and I are going to find the horseshoes! We've already found one, so don't worry.

☆ **TI:** So our readers shouldn't worry about the plans for the Midsummer Ball?

☆ **PS:** Oh no, everything will be perfect (she gulps) . . . I hope.

☆ **TI:** And what will you be wearing to the ball?

☆ **PS:** Oh, I've got the most gorgeous new sash to wear – it's pink and it sparkles like stardust in the moonlight! And I'll be wearing my tiara, of course. I can't wait!

THE ROYAL GAMES

By Tulip Inkhoof

Tomorrow marks the annual Royal Games and it should be a very memorable day. These games have been part of Chevalia's traditions for as long as this reporter can remember. Queen Moonshine and King Firestar will lead the royal procession from Stableside Castle to the royal box in the showground and then the games will begin! Here's a sneak preview of tomorrow's exciting events.

☆ **Dressage:** This event is always a popular one because it showcases the pinnacle of pony perfection! This year huge expectations are riding on newcomer Blossom, the young foal in a family of champion show ponies. Blossom is best friends with Princess Stardust, and all eyes will be on her debut performance. Can Blossom rise to the challenge or will she crumble under the pressure?

☆ **Showjumping:** We're expecting quite a competition in this year's showjumping arena. In last year's games, Sky Dancer took the title, but since she's decided to sit this year out to focus on her singing, the field is wide open. New jumps this year include the Volcano, a steaming reproduction of Chevalia's towering volcano, and the Pony Wings, an artistic creation honouring our special flying horse, Peggy. Be sure to cheer on the very best of Chevalia's jumpers!

☆ **Horseshoe-tossing:** It may look easy, but this is a game of great skill and concentration. Last year, a young pony called Bolt shocked everyone by coming from nowhere to win gold. Will she defend her title or is this event anyone's to win? Don't miss it!

☆ **Polo:** The polo match is a real favourite, with many ponies expected to come out to swoon over handsome Prince Storm. Storm usually prefers to muck around on the farms, but on the polo field he's a swift and graceful competitor.

☆ **Equestriathon:** This is the big event, the race around Chevalia. It's a strenuous, long-distance race all the way around our wonderful island. In the last games, Thunder took the title for the second year in a row. Will he do it again, or will we have a new gold medallist?

☆ **Closing entertainment:** Of course, not every pony loves the Royal Games for the sport! The day finishes with the most spectacular evening entertainment, including a grand banquet, dancing and a magical firework display.

Be sure to check back tomorrow for full coverage of all the fun at the Royal Games!